Recipe Ruckus

Don't miss a single

Nancy Drew Clue Book:

Nancy Drew
CLUE BOOK

#17

Recipe Ruckus

BY CAROLYN KEENE * ILLUSTRATED BY PETER FRANCIS

Aladdin
NEW YORK   LONDON   TORONTO   SYDNEY   NEW DELHI

ALADDIN

An imprint of Simon & Schuster Children's Publishing Division
1230 Avenue of the Americas, New York, New York 10020
First Aladdin hardcover edition March 2022
Text copyright © 2022 by Simon & Schuster, Inc.
Illustrations copyright © 2022 by Peter Francis
Also available in an Aladdin paperback edition.
ALADDIN and related logo are registered trademarks of Simon & Schuster, Inc.
NANCY DREW, NANCY DREW CLUEBOOK, and colophons
are registered trademarks of Simon & Schuster, Inc.
All rights reserved, including the right of reproduction in whole or in part in any form.
For information about special discounts for bulk purchases, please contact Simon & Schuster
Special Sales at 1-866-506-1949 or business@simonandschuster.com.
The Simon & Schuster Speakers Bureau can bring authors to your live event.
For more information or to book an event contact the Simon & Schuster Speakers Bureau
at 1-866-248-3049 or visit our website at www.simonspeakers.com.
Series designed by Karina Granda
Book designed by Heather Palisi
Interior designed by Tom Daly
The illustrations for this book were rendered digitally.
The text of this book was set in Adobe Garamond Pro.
Manufactured in the United States of America 0122 FFG
2 4 6 8 10 9 7 5 3 1
Library of Congress Cataloging-in-Publication Data
Names: Keene, Carolyn, author. | Francis, Peter, 1973– illustrator.
Keene, Carolyn. Nancy Drew clue book; 17.
Title: Recipe ruckus / by Carolyn Keene; illustrated by Peter Francis.
Description: First Aladdin paperback edition. | New York: Aladdin, 2022. |
Series: Nancy Drew clue book; 17 | Audience: Ages 6 to 9. |
Summary: When Nancy, Bess and George go searching for the perfect gift for the Drews'
housekeeper, Hannah, they choose a vintage apron, which may have belonged to a famous
local cook, and discover a recipe in the pocket—but when it disappears they have to
follow the clues to find out who stole it, and why.
Identifiers: LCCN 2021028809 (print) | LCCN 2021028810 (ebook) |
ISBN 9781534476899 (paperback) | ISBN 9781534476905 (hardcover) |
ISBN 9781534476912 (ebook)
Subjects: LCSH: Drew, Nancy (Fictitious character)—Juvenile fiction. |
Celebrity chefs—Juvenile fiction. | Vintage clothing—Juvenile fiction.
Theft—Juvenile fiction. | Detective and mystery stories. |
CYAC: Celebrity chefs—Fiction. | Vintage clothing—Fiction. | Stealing—Fiction. |
Mystery and detective stories. | LCGFT: Detective and mystery fiction.
Classification: LCC PZ7.K23 Ref 2022 (print) | LCC PZ7.K23 (ebook) | DDC 813.54
[Fic]—dc23
LC record available at https://lccn.loc.gov/2021028809

✱ CONTENTS ✱

Recipe Ruckus

Chapter

CLOTHES CALL

"Are you sure you feel okay, Nancy?" Bess asked. "If you have a fever, you should be in bed."

"I said I have *spring* fever," said Nancy with a smile. "That means I'm super excited for warmer weather, green trees, flowers—"

"Spring break," George Fayne cut in.

"Spring clothes," Bess said, striking a glam pose. "Like my brand-new spring jacket!"

Nancy and her two best friends were walking together up Main Street. It was the first week of spring break, so the usually busy street was busier than ever.

They had the same rules. They could walk up to five blocks from their houses as long as they were together. Since they were together most of the time, it was never a problem.

"Don't forget another awesome spring thing," Nancy said. "The River Heights Cherry Blossom Festival this Sunday."

"Who can forget with so many neat cherry blossom trees around?" Bess stopped to point at a tree sprouting fluffy pink buds.

"How did River Heights get so many of these trees in the first place?" George asked.

Nancy had just had this same conversation with her dad the day before, so she was happy to fill her friends in. "About a hundred years ago, the mayor of a Japanese town visited River Heights. He liked it here so much, he gave our mayor a gift of two dozen sakura."

"That's cool, I guess," George said, "but what about the cherry trees?"

Nancy giggled. "Sakura *are* cherry trees."

Bess scrunched her brow as she did the math. "Two dozen equals twenty-four," she said. "That's a lot of cherry trees."

"And since they were gifts, that's a lot of wrapping paper," George joked.

The girls relaxed under a tree for a few minutes, catching the falling blossoms in their hands. They laughed as they gently blew them at each other.

"Speaking of gifts," Nancy said as they

continued on their way, "that reminds me of my special mission today. I'm going to buy Hannah the perfect present for her birthday."

Hannah Gruen had been the Drews' housekeeper since Nancy was three years old. Like a mother, she made sure Nancy ate a good breakfast before school and did her homework after. Hannah also told the funniest jokes and baked the yummiest treats. Her birthday present had to be perfect. Just like Hannah!

"I have five dollars to spend on Hannah's present," Nancy said. "Any ideas?"

"How about five donuts from the Hole in One donut shop?" suggested George.

Nancy shook her head. "It's not a bad idea, but Hannah bakes even yummier donuts than the Hole in One."

"Then get Hannah something to use when she bakes," George said. "My mom uses tons of bowls for her catering business."

"Maybe."

Bess stomped her foot. "Maybe *not*! Instead

of a boring bowl, how about a blouse or a scarf? New clothes are always a perfect gift."

"Or old clothes!" George said.

"*Old* clothes?" Nancy asked.

George pointed down the block. "The sign outside the March of Time thrift shop reads 'vintage clothes for old-timey prices.'"

The girls approached the store window, which displayed gently worn clothes from years ago. There were pastel-colored cardigans embroidered with pearls, sky-high platform shoes— even a beaded dress trimmed with fringe.

"We were in this store before," Nancy said. "When we worked on a mystery."

"When *aren't* we working on a mystery?" Bess asked, smiling. "We're the Clue Crew!"

Nancy, Bess, and George loved solving mysteries and had their own detective club to prove it. They even had their own Clue Book where they wrote down all their suspects and clues.

"The owner of the store, Dulcie Yu, was a big help with our case," Nancy said. "Maybe she'll help me pick out a present for Hannah."

"We'll help too, Nancy," Bess said excitedly.

"*We* as in *me*?" George asked. She shook her head. "You know clothes aren't my thing."

"But *old* clothes are!" Bess said, nodding down at George's holey jeans and scuffed sneakers. "Which makes you an expert."

Nancy giggled. Bess and George were cousins, but they were as different as day and night. Bess had blond hair and blue eyes, and she loved new clothes and accessories. Dark-haired George loved accessories too, as long as they were for her tablet or computer.

"Okay, I'll help." George sighed. "But don't expect me to pick out anything pink or sparkly!"

When the girls entered the store, Dulcie was busy with a customer, so instead of being greeted by the owner, they were met by the musty smell of the vintage clothes hanging on racks and topping hat stands. Even the mannequins looked old-timey with their pencil-thin eyebrows and bright-red lips.

"How about this for Hannah?" Nancy asked, pulling a floral blouse from a rack.

"Too frilly!" George said, shaking her head. She began sifting through the blouses herself, nixing them one by one. "Too stripe-y . . . too itchy . . ."

"What do you like, Bess?" Nancy asked. She turned to find Bess gazing into a mirror as she tried on accessories.

"I am soooo liking this super cute hat! Have you ever seen a sun hat with a doll's head stuck on top?"

"Only in my nightmares!" George snapped. "Bess, take it off!"

"You may like it," Nancy said, grinning, "but it's not right for Hannah." She was about to turn back to the blouse rack when something next to Bess caught her eye—a white basket on the floor labeled APRONS.

"Hannah sometimes wears aprons when she cooks," Nancy said. "Maybe she could use a new one."

"You mean an old one!" Bess said with a wink.

The girls dug through the basket, pulling out aprons one by one. There was a white apron with yellow stripes, one with polka dots—even a barbecue apron that read DUDE WITH THE FOOD.

"Ooh, look at this one, Nancy," Bess said, holding up a light-blue apron. "It's got the prettiest red cherry design."

"Just in time for the Cherry Blossom Festival!" a voice said.

Nancy, Bess, and George turned to see Dulcie walking over. She looked springy herself in a vintage yellow dress and white Mary Jane shoes.

"I like the apron, Dulcie," Nancy said, taking it from Bess. "It looks familiar, but I can't remember where I saw it before."

"As long as it wasn't on Hannah," George said. She eyed the attached price tag. "And as long as the price is right."

Nancy leaned over to read the tag. "Five dollars. I'll take it."

"Sold to the girl with the strawberry-blond hair," Dulcie declared, striking a funny pose.

"Who did the apron belong to before?" Bess asked.

"I don't know," Dulcie admitted. "It was dropped off here a while ago along with other clothes. There was no name on the box." She held out her hand. "Why don't I ring that up for you?"

Nancy was about to hand over the apron when a buzz came from the back door.

"That must be the delivery I've been expecting," Dulcie said. "Wait right here while I sign for it."

As Dulcie headed to the back of the store, Nancy held up the blue apron. "It's perfect!" she said.

"Omigosh, it *is* perfect! Thanks, Nancy!"

Nancy gasped as she felt the apron being snatched from her hands. Whirling around,

she saw a familiar girl hugging it close to her chest. "Christy?"

"Christy Caruthers?" Bess added.

"Crafty Christy Caruthers!" George piped in.

Christy was in the other third-grade class at school. She was a whiz at making all kinds of crafts—even jewelry from paper clips and jelly beans!

"Why did you grab my apron, Christy?" Nancy asked.

"You didn't even say please!" added Bess, putting her hands on her hips.

"I said *thanks*. And it's not the apron I want."

Nancy was still confused. "Then what do you want?"

"This awesome cherry-design material. I'm going to make fabric flowers out of it to sell at the Cherry Blossom Festival on Sunday."

"You mean you want to cut it up?" Bess asked, horrified.

"Sure," Christy said with a shrug. "Snip, snip, hooray."

Nancy frowned at the thought of Christy cutting Hannah's present to shreds. "Can't you think of another craft project for the festival?"

"Like earrings," Bess suggested. "You could make them with spit-out cherry pits!"

"Gross!" Christy made a face. "That *idea* is the pits."

George tilted her head as she eyed the apron.

"If you think spit-out pits are gross, check out that crusty old dog-poop stain near the hem."

"D-dog poop?" Christy cried. "Ewww!"

As Christy dropped the apron, George shouted, "Quick, Nancy! Grab it!"

Chapter

POCKET-SIZED SURPRISE

Nancy snatched the apron out of the air before it hit the ground, then froze. "George? You weren't serious about the dog-poop stain, were you?"

"No," George said, doubling over.

Christy narrowed her eyes. "That means you tricked me . . . *Georgia* Fayne!"

"Uh-oh," Bess said under her breath.

George hated her real name more than she hated anything pink or glittery. Before things got any more heated, Nancy blurted out, "I found the apron first, Christy. It's a birthday present for someone special."

Dulcie smiled as she walked over to join the girls. "Nancy *did* find the apron first, but I'd be happy to help you find another pretty one."

Christy raised an eyebrow, then said in her frostiest voice, "No, thank you. I'm in a hurry, anyway."

Dulcie and the girls watched as Christy shoved open the front door, exiting the store in a huff.

Bess shook her head with a sigh. "I guess Christy will do anything for her crafts."

George bit her lip, then blurted, "Even if it means being crafty!"

The girls followed Dulcie to the counter, where she rang up the apron. After thanking Dulcie for her help, they tried on vintage sunglasses in geometric shapes before finally leaving the March of Time thrift shop.

Outside, George pointed to a rolling cart filled with old books. "I didn't know the March of Time sold books, too."

Nancy recognized a cookbook on the top shelf. The cover showed a picture of the famous cook Patty Crumbley. And tied around her waist was . . .

Nancy gasped. "The cherry-design apron! That's where I saw it before! On Hannah's Patty Crumbley cookbook!"

Nancy held up the apron so she could compare it to the one in the photo on the cookbook cover. They matched perfectly.

"Wow!" Bess exclaimed. "Do you think your apron used to belong to Patty Crumbley?"

"I don't think so, Bess," George said shaking her head. "There are probably millions of cherry-design aprons around."

"True," Nancy said, "but Hannah will still love this apron—even if it is one of a million!"

Bess jerked her head up. "If the apron is a hand-me-down, you should check the pocket before you give it to Hannah. There could be a yucky surprise like a used tissue or gum wrapper—"

"Or this!" Nancy said, pulling a small folded

piece of paper from the pocket. She handed the apron to George and carefully unfolded the yellowed sheet. "It looks like a recipe for chocolate chip cookies . . . with crushed-up pretzels!"

"Sweet and salty," said George. "Yum!"

"Double yum!" Bess exclaimed.

"I wish Hannah would bake these," Nancy said.

"Maybe she will," Bess said, excited. "Leave the chocolate chip cookie recipe in the apron pocket as a surprise!"

"Good idea! Except how do I keep Hannah from seeing the apron when I get home?"

"Or smelling it." Bess wrinkled her nose. "It does smell a little . . . old."

Nancy took a whiff, then made a face of her own. "How can I give Hannah a stinky apron?"

"It just needs airing out," George said. "I'll take the apron to my house and hang it up outside. You can pick it up later."

"Are you sure, George?" Nancy asked.

George nodded as she took the apron. "I've

smelled a lot worse. Like my sneakers after a soccer game."

"Eww!" Bess cringed.

"Speaking of baking and cooking," said Nancy, "Hannah's making tuna sandwiches for lunch. Can you both come over?"

"Yes, thanks," Bess replied. "Tuna sandwiches always taste better at someone else's house."

George sighed. "I've got to go. My mom's catering an office party today, and Dad is working at home. I promised to keep Scotty busy so Dad can have some peace and quiet."

"Peace and quiet with your three-year-old brother?" Bess laughed. "There's no such thing!"

George rolled her eyes. "I know. Save me a sandwich!"

When Nancy and Bess reached the Drew house, they found Hannah whipping up a batch of tuna salad. Propped up on the counter was the *Patty Crumbley Cookbook*!

"Guess what, Hannah?" Bess said. "We just

saw that cookbook on an old book cart at"—
Nancy nudged her in the ribs—"at the library!"

"It's my favorite cookbook," Hannah said.
"Especially since I found Patty's autograph inside
after I bought it."

"Really?" asked Nancy.

"Really. I'd show you, but I'm in the middle of following Patty's recipe for Tropical Tuna Salad."

"No wonder I smelled pineapples!" said Bess.

"What do you know about Patty, Hannah?" asked Nancy.

"I know that she lived in River Heights for a while," Hannah said as she mixed ingredients. "Her goal was to come up with one hundred recipes for chocolate chip cookies for a new cookbook she was writing."

Bess gasped. "One hundred?"

"Did Patty reach her goal?" Nancy asked.

"No one knows," Hannah said as she continued to stir the tuna salad. "I heard that Patty came up with ninety-nine recipes, but she died before she settled on the one-hundredth one."

Nancy and Bess traded looks. Patty Crumbley had lived in River Heights—and had a missing recipe for chocolate chip cookies?

"The one-hundredth recipe sounded tasty," Hannah went on. "People say it called for chocolate chips *and* crushed pretzels."

Bess's eyes went wide, and she covered her mouth with her hands.

"Chocolate chips," Nancy said slowly. "And—"

"Crushed pretzels?" Bess cut in.

"Interesting combo, huh?" Hannah said, wiping her hands on a towel. "I've got to get some more pepper from the pantry. No tasting before I get back."

Nancy nodded, still stunned. When Hannah was out of earshot, she turned to Bess. "The exact same apron!" she said breathlessly. "And a lost recipe for chocolate chip cookies with crushed pretzels!"

"Lost—and maybe found. Do you think the apron you bought really did belong to Patty Crumbley?"

"If it did, so did the one-hundredth recipe she came up with!"

"Whoaaaa!" Bess said under her breath.

Nancy eyes lit up at the possibility. "Think of the special things we can do with the missing recipe," she said in a hushed voice. "Donate it to a museum . . . or find Patty's family and surprise them with it!"

"Should we tell Hannah?" Bess asked.

Nancy shook her head. "The apron and the recipe are her birthday present. But let's go to George's house and tell her the awesome news."

"Okay," Bess said, "but only after lunch and those awesome Tropical Tuna Salad sandwiches!"

Nancy and Bess tried hard not to tell Hannah about the apron or recipe as they ate their lunch. The moment they finished, they headed straight to George's house.

As they turned onto George's block, they saw someone else they knew—Deirdre Shannon. Their classmate was walking quickly away from the Faynes'.

"What's Deirdre doing at George's house?" Bess asked in an almost-whisper. "They're not friends."

Nancy noticed Deidre clutching a crossbody bag. As she looked closer, she also noticed something else. . . .

"Why is Deirdre wearing a Pixie Scout shirt?" Nancy whispered. "She isn't a scout."

Deirdre didn't appear to see Nancy or Bess when she stopped to close her bag. She rolled her eyes as she struggled with a stuck zipper.

"It's one thirty," said Bess, glancing at her watch. "The Pixie Scouts usually have their meeting at three thirty on Fridays."

"It's spring break this week," Nancy pointed out. "They could have changed their schedule."

"Or their membership requirements," Bess replied. "Deirdre Shannon is *so* not the Pixie Scout type."

Nancy nodded. Pixie Scouts worked at being honest, trustworthy, and kind. Deirdre Shannon was pretty much the opposite of all of those things.

"It looks like Deirdre just put something in

her bag," Nancy whispered. "I wonder what."

Deirdre finally zipped her bag closed. She hadn't noticed Nancy and Bess when she hurried off in the opposite direction.

Nancy was still thinking about how strange Deirdre had been acting when she heard George's voice. She looked up just as her friend stepped outside.

"Hi, guys! Did you bring me a tuna sandwich?"

"We brought something better," Nancy said with a smile. "News about the cherry-design apron!" Nancy quickly filled her in about Patty Crumbley's missing recipe.

When she was done, George was gaping. "So the apron *was* Patty Crumbley's? The recipe too?"

"It sure sounds like it was!" Nancy confirmed.

"I want to see the apron and recipe again," Bess said. "Where did you hang Patty Crumbley's apron to air out, George?"

"It's on our cherry blossom tree in the corner," George replied with a grin. "Was that clever or what?"

Nancy and Bess followed George to the fluffy pink tree in the Faynes' front yard.

"I see lots of cherry blossoms," Bess said as they approached the tree. "No hanging apron, though."

George stopped walking abruptly and gulped. "Uh . . . neither do I," she said slowly. "Anymore."

"Anymore?" Bess asked.

Nancy turned to face George. "You mean it's gone? George, where is Patty Crumbley's apron?"

Chapter

BLOOM AND GLOOM

The girls raced over to the tree.

"I hung the apron right here on this branch," George said, pointing up. "I don't know why it's not here anymore!"

Nancy took a deep breath to calm herself down. "Maybe the wind blew it off."

"But I tied it tightly!" George insisted.

"Maybe it was a super strong gust," Bess suggested. "It could have blown the apron anywhere."

The girls searched around the tree and the

surrounding area. There was no apron on the ground or in the bushes or anywhere!

"It has to be around here," Nancy said. "George, think through the last hour. Where were you?"

"Up in my room playing with Scotty. My window doesn't face the front yard, so I wouldn't have been able to see the tree."

"Do you think your dad took the apron?" Nancy asked.

George shook her head. "Dad was in his home office for the last hour. I could hear his video-conference from my room."

"Maybe a squirrel took it," Bess suggested.

"Why would a squirrel need an apron, Bess?" George asked. "To bake nutty cookies?"

"I don't think the wind *or* a squirrel took the apron off the tree," Nancy said, "but somebody did."

"Somebody?" Bess repeated. "As in a person?"

"Who?" George asked.

Nancy reached into her pocket and pulled out

their Clue Book. "That's for us to find out, Clue Crew. Let's get to work!"

The girls sat under the cherry blossom tree, leaning against the trunk. Nancy opened the Clue Book and pulled out her favorite purple pen, which had been tucked inside.

"Okay. Let's figure out a timeline first," Nancy said. "When do you think Patty Crumbley's apron was taken off the tree?"

"I hung the apron on the tree as soon as I got home," George said. "That was a few minutes before noon."

"How do you know?" Nancy asked.

"When I went upstairs, Scotty was pointing to the clock, yelling, 'Both hands are on the twelve!' That's when his favorite show comes on."

Nancy drew a clock on the page with both hands on the twelve. "Then what did you do, George?" she asked.

"When the show ended, I left Scotty with Dad," George explained. "I saw you guys from his office window, so I came out to say hi."

"That was one thirty for sure," Bess said firmly. "I know because I looked at my watch."

Nancy drew a dotted line from the twelve to half past one, before looking up from the book. "The apron must have been taken between noon and one thirty. Now that we have a timeline, let's figure out who took it."

Nancy wrote the word "Suspects" on the next page. Underneath, she began their list with the number one.

"Who would want to take an old apron from a tree?" George asked. "Especially one that smells a little funky?"

"Crafty Christy Caruthers wouldn't mind," said Bess. "She wanted the fabric for her Cherry Blossom Festival project."

"Christy is definitely crafty enough to find a way to get it," George added. "She could have followed me all the way home!"

Nancy's eyes lit up. "I just thought of someone else: Deirdre Shannon."

"Why her?" George asked.

"Bess and I saw Deirdre walking away from your house when we were on our way over," Nancy explained.

George blinked hard. "You . . . did?"

Bess nodded. "Yeah, but why would Deirdre want the apron?"

"Uh, maybe because it wasn't the apron she wanted . . . ," George said slowly. "Maybe she wanted the chocolate chip cookie recipe in the pocket."

"The recipe?" asked Bess. "How would Deirdre even know about the recipe in the pocket?"

George sighed and hung her head. "Because I told her."

Nancy gaped at George. "You did what?"

Chapter

SMART COOKIES

"You told Deirdre about the recipe?" Bess was fuming. "Why would anyone tell Deirdre anything?"

"I ran into Deirdre on the way home," George explained. "She asked me about the apron, and I told her about Nancy buying it and how we'd found this delicious-sounding cookie recipe in the pocket." George shrugged. "I was hungry and must have had cookies on the brain. Deirdre asked if I was going to give the recipe to my mom."

"What did you tell her?" Nancy asked.

"That my mom didn't need a new recipe. She has a whole cookie-recipe file in her catering trailer."

Bess crossed her arms. "Then what happened?"

"I said goodbye to Deirdre and went to hang the apron on the tree."

"Did Deirdre see you do it?" asked Nancy, turning to face George.

"If she did, I didn't notice. Once the apron was on the branch, I went inside."

"I don't get it," Nancy said. "If Deirdre Shannon took the apron, why would she want a cookie recipe so badly?"

"Or a funky-smelling old apron?" added Bess. "Deirdre's always bragging about her new clothes on her blog. It is soooo annoying!"

"*Her blog!*" Nancy said, clapping her hands. "Let's go look at it right now."

"To look at clothes?" Bess asked.

"No, Bess," Nancy said, a grin slowly forming on her lips. "To look for *clues!*"

The girls raced into the Faynes' house, huddling around George's laptop as she pulled up *Dishing with Deirdre.*

"There's something about the Pixie Scouts," George said, pointing to the screen. "I wondered why she was wearing a Pixie Scout shirt."

"So did Nancy and I," Bess admitted.

Nancy leaned forward for a closer look. "It's an announcement for a Pixie Scout cookie-baking contest. The winning troop's cookie recipe will be the new Pixie Scouts cookies sold all across the country."

"*Cookies!*" George exclaimed. "Now we're getting somewhere!"

"It also says that the Pixie Scout troop with the winning recipe will be flown to Los Angeles, California, to be presented with a special cookie badge," Nancy said.

George frowned. "No wonder Deirdre joined the Pixie Scouts. She could become famous for the next Pixie Scout cookie flavor."

"By stealing Patty Crumbley's recipe!" said Bess, scowling.

"We won't know if Deirdre stole the recipe until we taste her troop's cookies to see if they have crushed pretzels in them," Nancy reasoned. She read the rest of the announcement. "The cookie contest is being held tomorrow in the River Heights Elementary School lunchroom. Five Pixie Scout troops from River Heights and the surrounding areas will be competing to represent the region."

Bess grabbed her friends' wrists. "We have to go to that contest tomorrow to look for clues—I mean taste for clues!"

Nancy added Deirdre's name to their list. With Christy Caruthers, they had two suspects.

"All this talk about cookies is making me want some," George said. "I wonder what Patty's other ninety-nine cookie recipes were like." She did a search for Patty Crumbley. Instead of her recipes, the FaceLook page for the River Heights Museum came up.

"Check it out," George said. "There's a special Patty Crumbley exhibit at the museum."

Nancy noticed a post from Horace Hudson, the museum's director. She read it out loud: "'We've just added something special to our Patty Crumbley exhibit. Hint: it's light blue, ties around the waist, and is *berry, berry nice!*'"

Nancy, Bess, and George traded stunned looks.

"Light blue, ties around the waist," Nancy said. "Sounds like an apron to me."

"But Mr. Hudson said 'berry, berry nice,'" Bess replied. "Not 'cherry, cherry nice.'"

George waved a hand in the air. "Berries,

cherries—close enough! If you ask me, that something special at the museum is the missing apron!"

Nancy studied the post. "Mr. Hudson wrote this only five minutes ago. He could have been here before one thirty easily."

"How would that Hudson guy know I had the apron?" George asked. "Or where to find it?"

"That's why we have to find him," Nancy insisted. "Next stop—the River Heights Museum!"

The biggest museum in River Heights was less than five blocks away from the Fayne house. It was also free on Fridays, so the girls were able to walk right in. The first person they saw was, by a stroke of luck, Horace Hudson, busy stacking brochures on the reception desk.

"Should we ask him about the apron?" Bess murmured.

"Not if we can *see* the apron first," Nancy whispered back. "Let's find the Patty Crumbley exhibit."

Nancy, Bess, and George hurried down the nearest hall. At the end was a wide canvas screen blocking a door with a sign reading: PATTY CRUMBLEY'S KITCHEN, OPENING SATURDAY.

"Saturday's tomorrow," Bess said. "I don't want to wait until tomorrow to see if Mr. Hudson's secret is the apron."

Nancy walked toward the screen. "Maybe we can peek in."

"Or sneak!" George said.

Nancy lunged forward to grab George's arm, but it was too late to stop her friend from slipping behind the screen into the exhibit. Nancy and Bess traded shrugs, then quietly followed her.

"Cool!" Nancy exclaimed as the trio looked around.

The Patty Crumbley exhibit was an old-timey kitchen, complete with a mint-green stove and matching fridge. In the middle of the kitchen was a big table with colorful bowls stacked on top.

"This looks exactly like Patty's kitchen on the cover of her cookbook," Nancy said.

"Great," George said looking around. "Now, where's Patty's apron from the cover of the cookbook?"

"There!" Bess blurted.

Where? Nancy looked to see where Bess was pointing. Sticking out of a closet door was a swatch of light blue material. Splashed across the material was a bright-red design.

"Good work, Bess," Nancy said excitedly. *"Cherry, cherry good!"*

Chapter

SCOOPER MARKET

Nancy wanted to see the whole apron. Bess pulled at the doorknob with one hand, then with both hands. "I think it's stuck," she said with a grunt.

"Let me try," said George.

Bess moved aside. George took hold of the knob. Gritting her teeth, she gave it a big pull and the door burst open. The girls stepped back slowly, their eyes wide.

Inside the closet was a woman, a light-blue apron tied around her waist.

"Do you see what I see?" Nancy whispered.

"It looks like Patty Crumbley," squeaked Bess. "I thought she was—"

"What's she doing in the closet?" George interrupted. She grabbed the side of the door and called, "Hey, Patty—"

CREEEEEAK!

Nancy, Bess, and George jumped to the side as the figure tipped out of the closet, and

landed face-first on the floor with a *CLUNK!*

"People don't clunk when they fall," said Nancy.

Bess nodded. "They plop. Or thud."

George kneeled down to get a closer look, turning the figure all the way around. "That's because this is a fake. It's one of those dress dummies like the kind Dulcie has at the March of Time."

"The dummy may be fake," Bess said with a smile, "but the apron is the real deal. Light blue with a flurry of cherries!"

Nancy lifted the material to study the design. "These cherries don't have stems," she pointed out. "Cherries aren't cherries without stems."

"That's because they're not cherries," a deep voice said.

The girls whirled around. Horace Hudson, the director of the museum, was standing near the screen, his hands on his hips.

"They're cranberries. As in cranberry sauce, cranberry muffins—"

"We know what cranberries are, thanks," George interrupted.

Nancy sighed. "We also know this isn't Patty Crumbley's apron."

"Phooey," Bess said, scowling.

"It certainly *was* Patty Crumbley's apron," Mr. Hudson said. "Patty, of course, owned many aprons."

"Okay. That makes sense," George said. "But what was a Patty dummy doing in the closet?"

Horace Hudson flinched. "We call it a *mannequin*."

"Manne-quin?" Bess asked.

"It's French for 'dummy,'" Mr. Hudson explained. He pointed to the mannequin of Patty. "The designers propped it up in the closet until they can find a stand to keep it steady."

"Oh." Nancy looked disappointed.

"Couldn't you girls wait until tomorrow to see the exhibit? You must be big Patty Crumbley fans."

"We're also detectives," Nancy said. "We were looking for Patty Crumbley's blue apron with the red cherry design."

"We had it," Bess added, "but now it's gone."

"You mean the apron from the cover of Patty's cookbook?" Mr. Hudson gasped. "It's almost as famous as Patty herself!" He grinned at the girls. "If you ladies find that apron, would you be willing to donate it to this exhibit? Please?"

Even though Nancy knew the apron was a gift for Hannah, she didn't want to disappoint Mr. Hudson either. "As soon as we find the apron, we'll let you know."

Mr. Hudson moved the screen so the girls could exit the exhibit.

After leaving the museum, Nancy opened the Clue Book to cross Mr. Hudson's name off their suspect list. "We have two suspects left," she pointed out. "Christy Caruthers and Deirdre Shannon."

"Who should we question next?" Bess asked.

"No one today," said George, looking at her watch. "It's getting late. I have to get home."

"Me too," Nancy replied. "I promised my dad I'd go food shopping with him."

"Maybe you can talk him into buying some ice cream," Bess said.

"Ooh! *Cherry* vanilla," Nancy said with a giggle.

The girls promised to meet the next morning to work on the case.

"Let's investigate Deirdre," George suggested. "The Pixie Scout cookie contest is tomorrow."

Nancy agreed. "That means doing a taste test."

"You mean a pop quiz," Bess said, trying not to smile.

"Pop quiz?" George asked, confused.

"Yup," Bess answered. "I'm going to *pop* those yummy cookies in my mouth!"

"And if we're lucky," Nancy added, "they'll have chocolate chips and crushed pretzels."

"Is this the cereal you like, Nancy?" Mr. Drew asked.

"My favorite! I'll put it in the cart."

Nancy and her dad were in the supermarket. As they walked up and down the aisles, she had plenty of time to tell him about the Clue Crew's new case.

"Anyway," Nancy said, reaching for the cereal, "Bess, George, and I think Deirdre Shannon is a great suspect."

"I understand why," Mr. Drew said, "but a good detective should always have plenty of evidence before accusing anyone, right?"

"Right, Daddy," Nancy said.

Mr. Drew wasn't a detective, but he was a lawyer. To Nancy, that was the next best thing—especially when he offered the Clue Crew the best advice.

"And . . . a good detective should always have enough ice cream," Mr. Drew added with a grin. "Agreed?"

"I totally agree!" Nancy replied.

"Why don't you head to the freezer and pick out a pint? I need to get some orange juice."

"Sure," Nancy said. "What flavor should I get?"

"Anything but bubblegum. I never know whether to eat it or blow bubbles."

"Oh, Daddy!" Nancy giggled. "I'll be right back!"

She made her way out of the cereal aisle. As she approached the freezer, she recognized two girls wearing Pixie Scout uniforms—Nadine Nardo and Shelby Metcalf. They were facing the opposite shelf, which was filled with baking supplies.

Nancy was about to say hi when she saw Nadine reaching for a bag of chocolate chips.

The cookie contest! Nancy thought. *Are they in Deirdre's Pixie Scout troop?*

Nancy wanted to hear what they were talking about. She quickly yanked the door of the

freezer open to hide behind. Shivering from a cold blast, she strained to listen in on Nadine and Shelby's conversation.

"Okay. These are the chocolate chips for our cookie recipe," Shelby said. "But are you sure

about that other ingredient? Really, truly sure?"

"I told you, Shelby," Nadine said with a groan. "Our troop's cookies are going to be sweet and *salty.*"

Nancy's jaw dropped.

Sweet and salty? Just like Patty Crumbley's missing recipe!

Chapter

CHEW CLUE

The next morning, the Clue Crew headed straight for the Pixie Scout cookie contest. Nancy couldn't wait to share what she had heard at the supermarket the night before.

"I know Nadine said salty," Nancy told her friends. "I heard her with my own ears."

"Did she have a bag of pretzels to crush in her basket?" asked Bess.

"I don't know," Nancy admitted. "Pretzels and chips are in aisle three. Nadine and Shelby were in aisle one." She gave a little shiver and added, "I was halfway inside an ice-cream freezer. Brrr!"

The Clue Crew reached River Heights Elementary School, which was open for the cookie contest, even though it was a Saturday during spring break.

Nancy, Bess, and George walked down the hall to the lunchroom where the judging was being held. At a table outside the door, a woman sat checking people in and giving out entry stickers to guests.

"Oh no," Nancy whispered. "How will we get in if we're not on the list?"

Just then, a girl wearing a full Pixie Scout uniform sat down at the table. The woman smiled as she gave her what looked like a copy of the list.

"There's a kid," George said. "Maybe she'll give us a break."

The Clue Crew cautiously approached the table. Nancy glanced at the girl's name tag. It read VIVIAN LENOX, OAKTOWN.

"Can I help you?" Vivian asked the girls.

"Hi," Nancy said, smiling. "We're here for the Pixie Scout cookie contest."

Vivian looked the girls up and down. "Why aren't you wearing your Pixie Scout uniforms? Or T-shirts?"

"We're not Pixie Scouts," Nancy explained. "We're here to—"

"Eat cookies?" Vivian snapped, narrowing her eyes at the girls. "I had a feeling you were cookie chasers."

"Cookie chasers?" George asked.

Vivian sat up a little straighter. "I've caught two cookie chasers in the last half hour. They wanted to sneak in and eat all of the cookies, but I stopped them!"

Bess nodded. "Is that why they put you in charge?"

"You bet!" Vivian pointed to one of her badges. "Where do you think I got this Truth Seeker badge? From a cereal box?"

"Are you one of the judges too?" Nancy asked.

"I wish," Vivian sighed. "The judge is

Gwendolyn Jackson. She's the Pixie Scouts' National Director of Cookie Affairs."

"And we're the Clue Crew!" Bess blurted out.

Nancy and George turned to stare at Bess. Why did she just tell Vivian that?

Vivian wrinkled her nose. "What's a Clue Crew?"

Bess leaned forward and whispered, "We're detectives sent here to help. We use our skills to catch cookie chasers in the act."

"No way!" Vivian blurted out, then continued more quietly. "You mean you're cookie-chaser chasers?"

"Shhh. Don't blow our cover," Nancy said, playing along. "We heard that a few cookie chasers slipped past you into the lunchroom."

Vivian gasped. "I missed them?"

"Don't worry, Viv," George said. "Nobody's perfect."

Vivian slapped three stickers onto the table. "Here. Go get them, Clue Crew!"

"Thanks," Nancy said as they took their stickers. "You can count on us."

Carefully fixing their stickers to their shirts, the girls walked past the table into the lunchroom.

"And we're in!" George declared.

"Good thinking, Bess," said Nancy as she glanced around the lunchroom. The space bustled with activity as Pixie Scouts and their leaders set up cookie plates on tables draped with long white tablecloths and banners identifying each troop's number and hometown. "Okay, where's the River Heights Pixie Scout troop?"

"Over there!" Bess said. "Shelby and Nadine are setting up their cookies."

Nancy looked to see where Bess was pointing, then spotted their classmates three tables away. Shelby and Nadine stacked cookies on a round plate while their leader, Mrs. Salazar, who also coached girls' soccer, stood to the side, talking to a few other girls.

"There's Deirdre," George said, nodding

across the room where the blogger turned Pixie Scout was standing alone adjusting her sash.

"How are we going to taste the cookies without Deirdre seeing us?" Bess whispered.

"River Heights Pixie Scouts!" Mrs. Salazar suddenly called out. "Gather round for a troop talk!"

Nancy, Bess, and George smiled as the Pixie Scouts, including Deirdre, crowded around their leader. The table and cookies were free!

"Are we lucky or what?" asked George.

Nancy nodded. "Let's taste those cookies to see if they have chocolate chips and crushed pretzels!"

The Pixie Scout troop was huddled so close, they didn't notice Nancy, Bess, and George inching up to their table.

"'Chip Chip Hooray'?" Nancy murmured, reading a sign next to the platter. "I don't remember seeing that cookie name on Patty's recipe."

"Hey, wait a minute," said George. "Chip Chip Hooray is the name of one of my mom's chocolate chip cookie recipes."

"It's probably a coinky-dink," Bess whispered. "Let's try them before the troop gets back."

Nancy, Bess, and George each grabbed a cookie. They were about to take bites when—

"Remember, girls! River Heights rules!" Mrs. Salazar shouted to her troop. "Now, let's show the judge what a cookie ought to taste like!"

While the Pixie Scouts high-fived, Bess whispered, "Oh no! Their meeting is over."

"We can't let them see us with their cookies," Nancy hissed. "Hide!"

Still holding the cookie, Nancy slipped under the table. Bess and George followed, letting the white tablecloth drop down to hide them.

The Clue Crew held their breaths as two pairs of feet appeared beneath the hem of their tablecloth tent. Nancy guessed they belonged to Mrs. Salazar and the judge, Gwendolyn Jackson.

Another pair of smaller feet wearing purple sneakers appeared alongside them, and then the girls heard Deirdre's voice.

"As everyone knows, I love to come up with new recipes, so it was awesome fun to bake these cookies."

George snorted. "Bake or *take*?"

Nancy froze as the talking outside the tablecloth stopped abruptly.

"Who said that?" Deirdre demanded.

The other scouts mumbled denials. Nancy turned to Bess and George.

"They're going to look under the table," Nancy whispered. "Eat the whole cookies—now!"

"Gladly!" Bess whispered.

The girls stuffed their cookies into their mouths. After a chew or two—

"Ewww!"

"Ugh!"

"Gross!"

Nancy squeezed her eyes shut. The cookies were salty—disgustingly salty.

But before she could get over the taste, Deirdre yanked up the tablecloth and glared at the girls. "Spies! Those three were spying on our cookies!"

Chapter

PIXIE PACT

Still sputtering, Nancy, Bess, and George came out from beneath the table.

"What were you girls doing under there?" demanded Ms. Jackson.

"You're not Pixie Scouts, are you?" Mrs. Salazar asked.

"I told you, they're spies," Deirdre said before the girls could answer. "That's why they were eating our cookies!"

Pixie Scouts and leaders from other troops

had begun drifting over. They wanted to see what the commotion was about.

Nancy made a face as she swallowed the last yucky crumb. "We're not spies. We're detectives."

George pointed to the plate. "And you call those cookies? They have more salt in them than the Atlantic Ocean!"

"Salt?" Mrs. Salazar cried.

Deirdre looked stunned. "How did so much salt get in our cookies?"

"As if you didn't know," George muttered.

Nancy glanced at the other five River Heights Pixie Scouts, who were silently exchanging knowing looks. Why didn't they look surprised too?

"Let me taste one," Ms. Jackson said. She grabbed a cookie and took a bite. Her eyes crossed and her face crumpled like a raisin. "Bleeeech! These *are* salty!"

Ms. Jackson turned to the scouts. "As National Director of Cookie Affairs, I'd like to

know how this cookie catastrophe occurred!"

"I told Deirdre about a recipe inside the pocket of an apron hanging on a tree in my yard," George explained.

"The recipe called for chocolate chips," added Bess. "And crushed pretzels."

"Pretzels?" Deirdre exclaimed. She turned to

the other scouts. "You didn't use pretzels in our recipe, did you?"

"Let's just say we added a pinch of salt," Nadine replied, grinning.

"Or a fistful," Shelby said.

"Are you serious?" Deirdre stomped her foot. "Why did you ruin Mrs. Fayne's recipe—" She clapped a hand over her own mouth as her eyes darted toward George.

"So that *was* my mom's recipe you used!"

"Mrs. Fayne's?" Mrs. Salazar asked. "Girls, you were supposed to come up with your own cookie recipe."

"We were going to come up with one," Nadine said quickly.

"Until Deirdre told us she sneaked into Mrs. Fayne's catering trailer," Shelby continued. "She found a cookie recipe, took it, and told us to use it instead."

The other scouts nodded in agreement.

"You wanted us to win, didn't you?" snapped Deirdre.

"Not like that!" Nadine said, throwing her arms up.

Nancy smiled at the Pixie Scouts. "I think I understand. You felt bad that Deirdre stole Mrs. Fayne's recipe, so you ruined it with tons of salt."

Shelby nodded. "Scouts are supposed to be honest. Stealing a cookie recipe is *not* honest."

"There wasn't enough time to come up with another cookie recipe," a scout with green-framed glasses added.

Mrs. Salazar turned to Deirdre. "Is what they're saying about Mrs. Fayne's recipe true?"

"Yes," Deirdre said with an eye roll. "I only joined the Pixie Scouts to win the contest and go to Los Angeles. I was going to ask Mrs. Fayne for some advice, but when George told me her mom kept the recipes for her super delicious cookies in her catering trailer, I decided it was easier to just take one."

"Deirdre, that's not the Pixie Scout way," Mrs. Salazar said. She turned to the other scouts.

"Neither is taking matters into your own hands before telling your troop leader."

All of the scouts murmured apologies. All except Deirdre.

"I never liked being a Pixie Scout, anyway," she said, whipping off her sash. "The T-shirts aren't fitted, and this sash clashes with my new sneakers!" She dramatically dropped the sash on the table as she declared, "I quit!"

Everyone watched as Deirdre marched toward the doors.

"I'll talk to her," Mrs. Salazar sighed.

"And I'll start the contest," Ms. Jackson said. "Without the salty cookies!" Then Mrs. Salazar and Ms. Jackson walked off in separate directions.

The Clue Crew turned to face the River Heights Pixie Scouts. "Thanks for sticking up for my mom's cookie recipe," George said. "Even if it meant messing it up."

"Thanks for putting up with Deirdre Shannon too," added Nancy.

Nadine groaned. "That was the hardest part!"

"Yeah," Shelby said. "There ought to be a badge for that!"

Nancy, Bess, and George waved goodbye and headed out of the lunchroom.

Vivian jumped up from her seat at the table and ran over. "So? Did you catch the cookie chaser?"

"More like the cookie *cheater*!" Nancy said.

As the Clue Crew left the school, Nancy took out the Clue Book and crossed Deirdre's name off the suspect list. "Deirdre didn't take Patty Crumbley's apron or her hundredth cookie recipe."

"Our next and final suspect is Christy Caruthers," Bess said. "She wanted to make fabric flowers out of Patty Crumbley's apron."

"Our next suspect will have to wait," stated George.

"Why?" Nancy asked.

Bess looked equally confused. "What else should we be doing?"

"Drinking smoothies!" George stuck out her tongue and made a face. "The only way to get this salty taste out of our mouths is with something sweet."

Nancy shook her head. "I spent five dollars on Hannah's birthday present yesterday. How can I buy a smoothie?"

"My treat!" George pulled out a gift card from Smoothie Susie's. "My dad got this for his birthday. He doesn't like smoothies, so he gave it to me."

"Thanks, George!" Nancy said, grinning.

Smoothie Susie's was on Main Street, just three blocks away. As the girls made their way up the street filled with shoppers, George whispered, "You guys! Look who's coming out of the craft store!"

Nancy turned toward the Craft Cottage shop. Walking out of the store and toward a parked car was . . .

"Christy Caruthers!" Nancy whispered.

"She's carrying a big shopping bag," Bess hissed. "I wonder what's in it."

George's eyes lit up. "*Peek*, and ye shall find. Let's help Christy into the car."

Christy looked surprised when Nancy, Bess, and George ran over. "Hi," she said. "What's up?"

"That bag you're carrying looks super heavy," George said. "Need help?"

"Not really," replied Christy. "Thank you anyway—"

"No problem!" George cut in as she grabbed the bag from Christy's hand.

"But I said—"

"And I've got the door!" Nancy added a little too cheerily as she opened the car's back door.

As Christy slipped into the back seat, Nancy saw George reading the receipt stapled to the bag. What was she looking for?

"I don't need help with my seat belt, Bess!"

Christy complained as Bess struggled to snap her in. "I'm not in preschool!"

"How sweet of you girls to help," Mrs. Caruthers called from the driver's seat. "Christy, you have the nicest friends!"

"I guess," Christy said sulkily. "Can I please have my bag back?"

"You got it," George declared. She leaned over to place the shopping bag on the car seat next to Christy.

"Bye!" Nancy said before shutting the door.

As the car drove off, Christy stared out the window, still looking baffled as Nancy, Bess, and George waved.

After the car turned the corner, Nancy and Bess rounded on George. "What was that all about?" Bess asked. "Why did we just treat Christy like the queen of England?"

"And why were you reading the receipt?" Nancy asked.

"Because Crafty Christy just bought a can of

spray glue, a large bag of sparkly beads, and five Styrofoam balls. Oh, and something else."

"What?" Nancy and Bess asked at the same time.

"Twenty wire stems," George replied. "And what goes with artificial stems?"

Nancy's eyes widened. *"Artificial flowers!"*

Chapter

STICKY SITUATION

"So Christy *is* making fabric flowers," Nancy said as she quickly wrote a note in the Clue Book. "And I'll bet she's using the fabric from Patty Crumbley's apron."

"Christy would have to cut up the apron to make the flowers," added Bess. "What if she cut up Patty's recipe too?"

"That's why we have to go to Christy's house now," Nancy replied.

"Before our smoothie break?" George cried. "If

I don't get this yucky taste out of my mouth—"

"Okay, smoothies first," Nancy said, snapping the Clue Book closed. "But the thought of Christy snipping the apron is leaving a bad taste in mine!"

Once at Smoothie Susie's, Bess insisted on sipping and sitting instead of sipping and walking to Christy's house.

"But we want speed, Bess," complained George. "Not accuracy!"

"Too bad. I don't want to drip smoothie all over my new spring jacket."

"Get a lid," Nancy suggested.

Bess shook her head. "Then I can't see what I'm sipping, and what's the fun in that?"

Forty minutes later, the girls were on their way. They knew that Christy lived in the bright-pink house on Acorn Street. It was known for its many wind chimes, which Christy had made herself.

The chimes tinkled as Nancy, Bess, and George walked across the porch to the front door. They

rang the bell a few times, but no one answered.

"It's a nice day," Nancy said. "Maybe the Carutherses are in the backyard."

Nancy, Bess, and George walked around the house, where they saw a wooden picnic table covered with craft supplies and, beside them, an open scrapbook.

"I love scrapbooks," cried Bess, running ahead. "Cool!" she called. "Christy wrote 'Best Party

Ever' on this page with pink glitter!"

"You know how I feel about pink and glitter," George said. "While you look at that, I'll look for the missing apron."

Nancy wanted to hunt for the apron too, but she was curious about Christy's pink glitter message. "I wonder whose party Christy meant."

"Here's the invitation," Bess said, pointing to the next page. "Sasha Molina had a birthday party at the bowling alley. Sasha's in our class. Why weren't we invited?"

Nancy was too busy reading the invitation to hear Bess's question. "The party was yesterday. At noon."

"So?" Bess still looked grumpy.

"So when Christy left the March of Time yesterday, she told us she was in a hurry," Nancy replied. "If it was Sasha's party she was hurrying to, she couldn't have been in George's yard taking Patty Crumbley's apron."

Bess's eyes lit up. "Patty Crumbley's apron went missing between noon and one thirty."

"Right!" Nancy said. "Christy didn't just have a party to go to—she had an alibi!"

"Oh yeah?" asked George. "Then how do you explain this?" When Nancy and Bess turned, George was holding what looked like a tall wire stem. Topping it was a blue fabric flower with a cherry design.

"Where did you find that?" Nancy asked.

George pointed across the yard. "It was with a bunch of other fake flowers laid out on a towel on the grass."

Nancy felt her heart sink. So much for Christy's alibi. "Christy did cut up Patty Crumbley's apron to make the flowers. And probably the recipe too."

"I told you we'd be too late," George said, glaring at her cousin. "And all because Miss Fine Dining had to sip her smoothie sitting down!"

Bess didn't respond. She was too busy examining the flower in George's hand. She took a big whiff.

"What are you doing, Bess?" Nancy asked. "You know that flower isn't real."

"It's not Patty Crumbley's apron, either," said Bess. "This flower smells fresh and new, not old and musty."

George leveled the flower with her nose. "I just noticed something else. This fabric has red cherries and tiny yellow dots."

"There were no yellow dots on Patty's apron," Nancy said. "Let's make sure the other flowers have dots too."

The girls walked across the yard, where the other fabric flowers laid neatly on a towel. All of them had the same small yellow dots. Nancy was about to point them out when—

Crunch!

Nancy, Bess, and George knew that sound. It was a car pulling up a gravelly driveway.

"It sounds like the Carutherses are back," Nancy said. "I don't want Christy to find us going through her stuff."

"Put down the flower, George," Bess ordered as she backed away from the towel. "Quit fooling around," she snapped when George wiggled her hand, still clutching the stem.

"Uh . . . I would if I could. But I can't."

"Why not?" Nancy asked, increasingly frantic.

"Because," George said, shaking her hand even harder, "*it's stuck*!"

Chapter

SPOT ON

"What do you mean *it's stuck*?" Nancy demanded.

She tried to pull the stem from George's hand—only to get stuck herself!

"We don't have time for jokes," Bess snapped. "Here. Give me that!"

Bess grabbed the stem above Nancy's and George's hands. When she tried to open her own hand— "Oh no!" she cried. "Now I'm stuck too. Ugh!"

"Nancy? Bess? George?" a voice cried.

The girls turned to see Christy gaping at them.

"What are you doing?"

"What we always do," Nancy said, forcing a smile. "Sticking together."

"That's what glue's supposed to do," Christy said. "Before my mom drove me to the library to return a book, I sprayed all of my flower stems with it."

"Why?" Bess asked.

"So I could glue green glitter on them," Christy said. "I thought the stems would dry before I got back."

"They dried . . . on us," Nancy said.

"No problem," Christy said, giggling. "I have something that'll unstick you. It's safe and one hundred percent natural." She reached into a bin under the picnic table for a bottle of Goop Goodbye, then squirted it on the girls' hands, freeing them from the stem. "Now, what were you doing in our backyard going through my crafts?"

"We were looking for the blue apron with the cherry design," Nancy admitted. "The one you really wanted at March of Time yesterday."

"George hung it up in her yard," Bess explained, "and now it's gone."

Christy planted her hands on her hips. "So you thought I stole it?"

"Not anymore," Nancy said quickly. "We saw in your scrapbook that you went to a birthday party yesterday."

"You were snooping through my scrapbook too?" Christy cried. "Why?"

"Because," George blurted out, "we think you should have your own show on YouView!"

Christy stared at George, her expression softening. "Me? What kind of show?"

"A crafts show, of course," replied Nancy. "You can call it *Crafty Christy*."

"It's what everyone calls you anyway," Bess said, before getting a nudge from Nancy.

"Crafty Christy," Christy repeated, smiling. "I like it. . . . I like it a lot."

Christy picked up a fabric flower and held it out. "Take a flower. It's my way of saying thanks for your awesome idea!"

Nancy, Bess, and George stared at the flower. The stem still looked kind of sticky.

"Um . . . no thanks, Christy," Nancy said.

"We're the Clue Crew," added Bess. "Not the *Glue Crew*!"

The girls said goodbye to Christy. As they walked up Acorn Street, George said, "Cross Christy's name off the suspect list, Nancy. She's clean."

"Christy may be clean," said Bess, "but look what the stuff she sprayed did to my new spring jacket!"

Nancy and George turned to see Bess staring at her sleeve, where there was now a big blue spot.

"Too bad, Bess," Nancy said. "Maybe it'll come out in the wash."

"My mom is always getting food spots off clothes and tablecloths for her catering job," said George. "She uses a detergent called Stain, Stain, Go Away."

"My parents don't have that," Bess sighed.

"You're in luck! Mom and Dad collect dirty clothes on Friday and do laundry on Saturday."

"Saturday's today," Bess said. "Do you think they'd wash my jacket too?"

George grinned. "If we hurry and make the next load."

The girls were speeding toward George's street when a thought made Nancy stop suddenly. "Wait!" she shouted.

"What, Nancy?" George asked.

"If your mom and dad collect dirty clothes to wash on Friday, could the apron have been collected too?"

"You mean one of them took it off the tree?" George asked.

"Ooh!" Bess said excitedly. "That means the missing apron could be in the washer!"

Nancy was feeling hopeful again, until another thought flashed into her head. A *terrible* thought.

If the apron was in the washer, so was something else!

Clue Crew—and
YOU!

Ready to think like Nancy, Bess, and George and help solve the case of Patty Crumbley's missing apron? Write your answers down on a separate piece of paper, or read on to see what happened!

1. The Clue Crew ruled out Deirdre Shannon, Horace Hudson, and Christy Caruthers. Who else could have taken Patty Crumbley's apron?

2. Nancy thinks the missing apron might be in the Faynes' washer, but she's worried something else is in there too. What do you think it could be?

3. Bess used her sense of smell to rule out Christy's fabric flowers. Which other senses—touch, sight, hearing, and taste— did the Clue Crew use to help solve this mystery?

Chapter

PAPER CAPER

"What's wrong, Nancy?" Bess asked. "Your smile turned into a frown really quickly."

"I just thought of something horrible. If Patty Crumbley's apron is being washed, so is her one-hundredth cookie recipe!"

"Sudsed and spinned to smithereens!" George exclaimed. "What should we do?"

"Maybe we can rescue Patty's apron and the recipe," Nancy said hopefully. "Maybe your parents haven't tossed it in the washer yet."

The Clue Crew ran all the way to the Fayne house. Their feet thundered down the stairs to the laundry room in the basement. They stared at the soapy load tumbling inside the washer. Something light blue with a cherry design was tumbling too!

"It's Patty's apron," Nancy sighed.

Bess forced a smile. "At least it won't smell funky anymore," she said. "The apron will be squeaky-clean."

"So will the recipe in the pocket," muttered George. "Like a hard-boiled rock of papier-mâché!"

"Unless we stop the washer," Nancy said hopefully. "Do you know how to do that, George?"

"I'll find out." She turned toward the staircase and shouted up, "Mom or Dad! Please come down quick!"

In seconds, Mrs. Fayne hurried down the stairs. "What's wrong?"

"We want to stop the washer, Mrs. Fayne," Nancy said. "Please?"

"The washer can't be stopped unless I pull the plug, Nancy," explained Mrs. Fayne.

"And I really don't want to do that."

"But we have to get the apron out, Aunt Louise," Bess pleaded. "The blue one with the cherry design."

"Oh, is that yours? I saw it hanging on the tree yesterday and took it down for a wash."

"I thought you were at a job yesterday, Mom," George said.

"I was, but I came home to get a sweater. When I saw the apron, I thought it was from a neighbor. They sometimes leave me items they think might be useful for my catering jobs. It smelled a little musty, so I dropped it in the laundry basket yesterday to throw in the wash."

Nancy sighed. "Along with the recipe in the pocket."

"A recipe? So that's what I pulled out of the pocket."

"You mean you found it, Aunt Louise?" Bess asked.

"I found a small blank scrap of paper," Mrs.

Fayne replied. "I guess the recipe was written on the other side."

Nancy was so happy, she could do cartwheels. The apron was in the washer, but the recipe wasn't. "What did you do with the paper, Mrs. Fayne?" she asked.

"Tell us, Mom. Please!" George said.

"I tossed it in Scotty's scrap bin," Mrs. Fayne said. "I put all unused scraps of paper there for him to draw on so he doesn't draw on the walls."

"Thanks, Mrs. Fayne!" Nancy said with a smile. "We'll explain everything soon." She turned to George. "But first, take us to Scotty's scrap bin."

George led the way up to her brother's room. The girls filed through the door, then froze. Scotty was holding a scrap of paper in one hand . . . and a pair of safety scissors in the other!

From where they stood, Nancy recognized Patty Crumbley's writing. "Scotty's got the recipe! And he's about to cut!"

"Don't do it, Scotty!" George warned as she held out her hand. "We need that paper. Now."

Scotty tilted his head. "What's the magic word?"

"Please!" Bess shouted.

"No!" Scotty shouted back. "I want to make paper spaghetti and clay meatballs!" He eyed the recipe. "Should I cut it this way . . . or that way . . . or . . ."

"George, do something!" cried Nancy.

"There's only one thing to do with Scotty." George sighed. "Time to make a deal!"

George walked over to Scotty, who was seated at a little red table. "Give me the paper, and I'll read you a story every night until your next birthday."

"*Two* books a night!"

"One," George said firmly.

Scotty narrowed his eyes. "Two!"

Nancy and Bess traded worried looks. Scotty was going to be a tough nut to crack!

"Two, huh? Well, I could tell Mom you plucked *two* strawberries off the strawberry shortcake she baked when she wasn't looking—"

"Okay, one book!" Scotty cut in. "But when you read, you have to do your funny voices!"

"Deal." George held out her hand. "Paper, please."

Nancy and Bess breathed a collective sigh of relief as Scotty dropped Patty Crumbley's one-hundredth recipe into George's palm.

While Scotty began rolling clay meatballs, the girls examined the rescued scrap.

"'Chocolate chip cookies with crushed pretzels'!" Nancy read, relieved. "It's Patty Crumbley's one-hundredth recipe!"

"Sweet!" Bess exclaimed.

"And salty!" Nancy grinned. "Good work, Clue Crew!"

"Nancy, this is the nicest birthday present I ever received," Hannah said, holding up the blue apron with the red cherry design. "And I can't believe it's vintage. It's so crisp and—"

"Clean?" Nancy asked.

"We made sure of that, Hannah!" Bess giggled.

Nancy had invited Bess and George to Hannah's pancake breakfast. Nancy's Labrador puppy, Chocolate Chip, wagged her tail as she hungrily watched Mr. Drew flip pancakes at the stove.

"Does the apron look familiar, Hannah?" Nancy asked.

"Familiar?"

Nancy picked up Patty Crumbley's cookbook and held it high. "Ta-daaa!"

"Well, how do you like that?" Hannah said, surprised. "It looks just like the one Patty Crumbley wore."

"That's because it *is* Patty Crumbley's, Hannah," Nancy said excitedly. "Look in the pocket!"

Hannah reached into the apron pocket and pulled out the scrap of paper. "What's this?" she

asked, looking it over. "A recipe for chocolate chip cookies?"

"Not just any recipe, Hannah," Nancy said. "It's *Patty Crumbley's one-hundredth cookie recipe*."

"The one that was never found!" Bess added.

"Until we found it!" George said proudly. "Boom!"

Hannah's mouth hung open. Even Mr. Drew came over to check it out.

"This is amazing," Hannah finally managed to say.

"Are you sure the recipe was Patty's?" Mr. Drew asked.

Nancy looked at Bess and George. They were sure the chocolate chip cookie recipe was Patty's, but how could they be extra sure? Suddenly, an idea clicked into place.

"Hannah, let's look at your cookbook," Nancy said. "You said Patty signed it. Can you open to the signature, please?"

Hannah flipped the cookbook open. Nancy held the recipe against Patty Crumbley's autograph. The handwriting wasn't just similar, it was . . .

"A perfect match!" Nancy declared. "How do you like your birthday present now, Hannah?"

"I think it's so special, we should do something special with it. Maybe we can find Patty's family and share it with them."

"And with Horace Hudson," Nancy said. She explained everything about the Patty Crumbley exhibit at the River Heights Museum.

"Great idea," Hannah declared. "Until we find Patty's family, we'll share it with the museum."

"The recipe too, Hannah?" asked Bess.

"Not yet," Hannah said, grinning mischievously. "I think I'll bake Patty Crumbley's recipe for the Cherry Blossom Festival today."

"Her *one-hundredth* recipe!" Nancy announced happily.

George gave a little whistle. "One hundred cookie recipes. No wonder Patty Crumbley was famous."

"Do you think the Clue Crew will ever solve one hundred mysteries, Nancy?" Bess asked.

Nancy smiled. "As long as we stick together," she replied, thinking of the sticky flower stem. "And we know we can do *that*!"

Test your detective skills with even more Clue Book mysteries:

Nancy Drew Clue Book #18: Bird Bonanza

"I'm a Bluebird," Nancy announced. It was the first day of Bird Bonanza Camp at the River Heights Nature Park. Nancy had found her name on the list at the sign-in station in the Welcome Center. Next, she ran her finger down the page, looking for Bess Marvin and George Fayne, her two best friends. "We're all on Team Bluebird," Nancy reported happily. Bess and George squealed with delight.

"Here's the plan," said George. She whipped a calculator out of her back pocket. "If we each learn to identify five new birds per day . . . that's five times three . . ." She stuck out her tongue as she punched the numbers on the keypad.

"We know you want to win the Big Bird Count raffle prize," Bess said, narrowing her eyes at George. The girls were cousins as well as friends. "But I'm here for bird-watching, not bird-counting."

"The top prize in the Big Bird Count is a pair of PowerTron 5000s," George gushed. "You can practically see to the moon with binoculars that strong. I have to win!" George had a pile of electronic gadgets at home, but she could never get enough.

"It's not a contest," Nancy reminded her. "It's a raffle. Everyone who participates in the Big Bird Count gets their name entered. You have as good a chance as anyone to win."

George groaned. "But I don't know the names of many birds. You have to know what the birds are called for your numbers to count."

"That's what Bird Bonanza Camp is for." Bess held up a small bird-guide booklet she had tucked in the outside pocket of her lunch cooler. She liked to be super prepared for every adventure. "Nancy and I will quiz you. We'll describe a bird, and you can guess what kind it is."

"We'll all learn together." Nancy's blue eyes twinkled.

"That plan is for the birds—in a good way." George grinned.

"Let's go grab our swag bags," suggested Bess. She pointed to a swarm of campers crowded around a table on the other side of the room. The kids were all wearing baseball caps in different colors—red, orange, yellow, and black. "I think our team hats are in those bags."

As the girls made their way over to the swag bag station, three black-capped Chickadees moved away and Nancy, Bess, and George took their spots. The table was piled high with Bird Bonanza backpacks, each with a camper's name on it.

"I found mine," said Nancy. She pulled out a blue cap and placed it on her head, threading her reddish-blond ponytail through the small opening at the back. Then she stowed her lunch bag inside her new backpack.

"I can't find mine," George complained.

"Do I need the Clue Book?" Nancy asked. She patted her back pocket, where she kept the special notebook she shared with her friends. They used it to write down suspects and clues when they had a big mystery to solve. The third-graders were the best detectives at River Heights Elementary School. They'd even formed a club called the Clue Crew.

"Mystery solved. I found it," Bess called. Her blond waves peeked out from under her blue hat as she handed the bag to her cousin. "They wrote your real name on it—*Georgia*." Bess smirked. She knew how much George hated her real name.

"No one better call me that. That's all I have to say," George grumbled as she yanked her cap sideways on top of her dark curls. She and her cousin put their lunch bags in their new swag bags and zipped them up.